MW01154130

The Pawnee Nation

by Anna Lee Walters

Consultants:
Debra D. Echo-Hawk, Director of Education and Training
Rebecca S. Eppler, Assistant, Education and Training
Pawnee Nation of Oklahoma

Bridgestone Books
an imprint of Capstone Press
Mankato, Minnesota

J 970

Bridgestone Books are published by Capstone Press
151 Good Counsel Drive, P.O. Box 669, Mankato, Minnesota 56002
http://www.capstone-press.com

Library of Congress Cataloging-in-Publication Data
Walters, Anna Lee, 1946-
    The Pawnee Nation/by Anna Lee Walters.
    p. cm.—(Native peoples)
    Includes bibliographical references and index.
    Summary: An overview of the past and present lives of the Pawnee Nation including their history, food and clothing, homes and family life, religion, music, and government.
ISBN 0-7368-0501-X
    1. Pawnee Indians—History—Juvenile literature. 2. Pawnee Indians—Social life and customs—Juvenile literature. [1. Pawnee Indians. 2. Indians of North America—Great Plains.] I. Series.
E99.P3 W35 2000
978'.004979—dc21   99-053063

Editorial Credits
Rebecca Glaser, editor; Timothy Halldin, cover designer; Sara A. Sinnard, illustrator;
  Kimberly Danger and Katy Kudela, photo researchers

Photo Credits
Debi Gover, 14
Kansas State Historical Society, Topeka, 10
Nebraska State Historical Society, 8
Pawnee Nation of Oklahoma/Education Department, cover, 6, 16, 18, 20, 22
Ralph Haymond, 12

1 2 3 4 5 6 05 04 03 02 01 00

Table of Contents

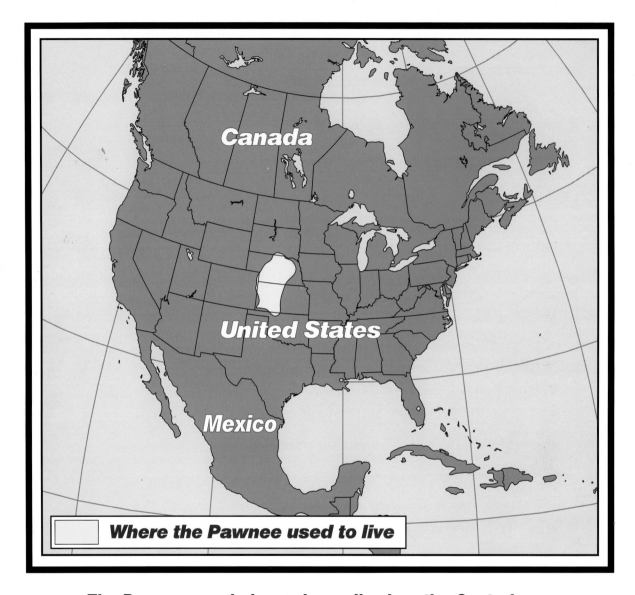

Where the Pawnee used to live

The Pawnee people have always lived on the Central Great Plains of North America. They once lived where the states of Kansas and Nebraska are now. Today, many Pawnee live on the Pawnee Reservation in Pawnee, Oklahoma.

Fast Facts

Today, the Pawnee people live like many other North Americans. But many remember their traditional ways of life. These facts tell about Pawnee life in the past and today.

Lodging: The Pawnee used two kinds of houses. Mud lodges were the Pawnee's main homes. Pawnee used tipis when they hunted buffalo. Today, most Pawnee live in modern houses.

Food: The Pawnee's main food was buffalo meat. The Pawnee also grew corn, squash, and pumpkins.

Clothing: Women sewed soft, long-lasting clothes and shoes from animal hides. They decorated their clothing with beadwork, fringe, and paint. Today, the Pawnee still make and wear this type of clothing for special occasions.

Language: The Pawnee people have always had their own language. Some Pawnee still speak the Pawnee language today. The Pawnee language belongs to the Caddoan language family. Plains Native American groups speak Caddoan languages.

Special Event: Every year, the Pawnee hold a Homecoming Powwow the first weekend in July. The Pawnee come together and visit during this celebration.

The Pawnee People

Today, the Pawnee people have their own land in Oklahoma. Many Pawnee live on the Pawnee Reservation. Some Pawnee live in towns and large cities.

The Pawnee have lived on the plains for centuries. Old Pawnee villages still exist in Kansas and Nebraska. The Pawnee lived in these areas for more than 200 years.

The Pawnee have always called themselves a nation. Four bands make up the Pawnee Nation. These four groups are Chaui, Kitkehaki, Pitahauerat, and Skidi. All of these bands speak the Pawnee language.

At one time, Pawnee children did not go to school. Their families taught them the Pawnee way of life. Today, all Pawnee children go to school. Many Pawnee go to college.

Pawnee wear traditional clothing at powwows. Many powwows take place on the Pawnee Reservation.

Pawnee Scouts

In 1864, the U.S. Cavalry asked the Pawnee to help locate and fight other Native American groups on the plains. The Pawnee agreed. They formed a group called the Pawnee Scouts. The group was successful. In 1867, the U.S. government asked the Pawnee to guard railroad construction workers. The Pawnee Scouts served until 1877. Only one Pawnee Scout died in all of the group's years of service.

Pawnee History

Before Europeans came to Pawnee lands, each Pawnee band had its own village and its own leaders. The leaders decided where to build villages. The Pawnee built many of the old villages on high bluffs near rivers or creeks. The people could see for miles around them.

Pawnee leaders kept the people safe and well. The village leaders told the people when to hunt and when to plant crops. Some leaders acted as priests or doctors for the people.

Spanish explorers came to Pawnee lands in the 1500s. In the 1800s, many Europeans settled on Pawnee lands. The Pawnee did not fight with the Europeans. But the U.S. government forced the Pawnee to stay on small reservations in Nebraska.

In the 1870s, the U.S. government moved the Pawnee to the Pawnee Reservation in Oklahoma. The Pawnee have lived on the reservation for more than 100 years.

Pawnee Homes

The Pawnee built homes to be safe from the weather of the plains. They built large round houses called mud lodges. From a distance, mud lodges looked like small hills. The lodges were safe from tornadoes because they were set into the ground. They were safe from floods because they were built on hills.

Many people helped make a mud lodge. They cut poles from trees. They dried the poles. They then set the dry poles in the ground and covered them with mud and dirt. The Pawnee built mud lodges in permanent villages.

The Pawnee set up tipis in camps when hunting buffalo. The Pawnee made these cone-shaped homes by tying poles together at the top. They covered the poles with hides or canvas. Tipis were easy to move.

Today, the Pawnee live in modern houses that have electricity and water. But they still build mud lodges and tipis on the Pawnee Reservation. The Pawnee use these homes for special events.

Before Europeans arrived, the Pawnee lived in villages in Kansas and Nebraska. The mud lodges looked like small hills from a distance.

Pawnee Food and Clothing

The Pawnee once were self-sufficient. They could find everything they needed on the land. Today, Pawnee shop in stores for food and clothing.

In the past, the Pawnee hunted buffalo and other animals. They ate fish and some types of birds. They also planted their own variety of corn. The Pawnee ate the ears of corn as well as the corn stalks.

The Pawnee saved corn in several forms to eat during winter and other hard times. They made corn bread. The Pawnee cooked and dried corn to make hominy. This grain was valuable because it could be saved for a long time.

The Pawnee made clothes from the hides of animals they hunted. The Pawnee decorated the clothes with beadwork, fringe, and painted designs. They made leggings, shirts, dresses, blankets, and shoes. Today, the Pawnee still make some clothing by hand to wear on special occasions.

The Pawnee still wear fringed and beaded clothing for special occasions such as the Pawnee Homecoming.

Pawnee Families

Pawnee life centers around the family. The Pawnee believe that families must have unity. Families must work together and be kind to one another. The Pawnee believe that families make up the strength of a band. All the bands must be strong to make a strong Pawnee Nation.

Families are important because each family is a part of the Pawnee history. Families sometimes record their history in songs. They celebrate their histories at certain times of the year. They hold dances and sing songs about family members who are no longer living.

Most Pawnee think of their tribe as one big family. In the tribe, they call each other mother, father, sister, brother, aunt, uncle, grandma, or grandpa. Pawnee children have many grandmas, grandpas, aunts, and uncles because of this belief.

Pawnee life centers around the family. These cousins attended a powwow together.

Pawnee Religion

The old Pawnee religion came from what the Pawnee observed in the natural world. The Pawnee thought of the world as a big house. They thought everything in nature made up a large family. The Pawnee believed that a great creator made this house and the family. The Pawnee spoke and sang to that creator.

The Europeans thought the Pawnee did not have a religion. They brought Christianity to the Pawnee. Christianity is a religion that follows the teachings of Jesus Christ. Today, many Pawnee remember the old religion. But most Pawnee are Christians. A few Pawnee practice both religions.

Today, many Pawnee belong to the Native American Church. The church conducts prayer meetings for worship and special occasions. Special meetings are held for holidays, birthdays, and physical or spiritual healing. Meetings also may be held to bless children in school or to address special requests.

The Pawnee chapter of the Native American Church holds activities in the Pawnee community building. The church is one of the most active organizations of the Pawnee Nation.

Pawnee Music

Music is an important part of Pawnee social gatherings. The Pawnee believe language and voice have power. At one time, they thought everything in the universe had a voice. Nature seemed to speak to the Pawnee.

At Pawnee gatherings, the men sit around a large round drum. They form two circles when there are many singers. Each man has a drumstick to hit the drum. Women sit in rows behind the men. They sing songs that are centuries old. They also sing new songs.

The Pawnee sing songs about almost everything in the universe. The songs tell what the creations in the universe say to the Pawnee. The songs tell of people who do wonderful things. They also help the Pawnee people remember the words and actions of past Pawnee heroes.

Music is an important part of Pawnee social gatherings, such as this youth dance.

Pawnee Government

The Pawnee have a written constitution. The constitution sets up a judicial system and laws. Pawnee people must agree to live by the laws in their constitution. The Pawnee Nation's Bill of Rights states that the Pawnee have freedoms of worship and speech.

The Pawnee elect two councils of leaders. Each council has eight members. The Pawnee Business Council represents the entire Pawnee Nation. It is the main governing body of the Pawnee Nation. The Nasharo leaders represent the Pawnee bands. Two members from each band make up the Nasharo Council.

Long ago, Pawnee laws were passed through the spoken word from one generation to the next. There was no written constitution. The Pawnee consider their constitution to be very important. They believe it helps them be better citizens of the Pawnee Nation and of the United States.

This seal represents the Pawnee government. Plains Indians called the Pawnee "wolves" because the Pawnee were courageous.

Hands On: Make a Corn Decoration

Pawnee stories tell how corn was important to the Pawnee people. The Pawnee often decorated corn and placed it in special locations in their homes. You can make a corn decoration for your home.

What You Need

About 240 plastic "pony" beads
1/2-inch (1.3-centimeter) thick
    craft foam
Beige-colored paper
Ribbon
Craft glue
An adult to help

What You Do

1. Ask an adult to help you cut the foam into the shape of an ear of corn. It should be about 6 inches (15 centimeters) long and about 1 inch (2.5 centimeters) wide.
2. Squeeze a line of glue onto the foam. Press the beads sideways into the glue. Make neat rows of beads until the foam is covered. The foam and beads make an "ear" of corn.
3. Cut the beige paper into wide, pointed strips. These are the husks. Glue the ear of corn on top of the husks.
4. Gather the top of the husks and tie with the ribbon.
5. Place your decoration in your home.

Words to Know

cavalry (KAV-uhl-ree)—soldiers who fight on horseback
council (KOUN-suhl)—a group of leaders
judicial system (joo-DISH-uhl SISS-tuhm)—courts that enforce laws
lodging (LOJ-ing)—a place to live
material (ma-TEER-ee-uhl)—the things from which something is made
religion (ri-LI-juhn)—a set of spiritual beliefs people follow
self-sufficient (self-su-FIH-shent)—to meet a person's or a group's own needs
unity (YOO-ni-tee)—a condition of agreement

Read More

Lacey, Theresa Jensen. *The Pawnee.* New York: Chelsea House, 1996.
Sita, Lisa. *Indians of the Great Plains: Traditions, History, Legends, and Life.* Philadelphia: Courage Books, 1997.

Useful Addresses

**The Oklahoma Historical
  Society**
2100 N. Lincoln Boulevard
Oklahoma City, OK 73105

**The Pawnee Nation of
  Oklahoma**
P.O. Box 470
Pawnee, OK 74058

Internet Sites

National Museum of the American Indian
http://www.si.edu/nmai
Pawnee Information
http://www.pawnee.com/indian
Pawnee Literature
http://indians.org/welker/pawnee.htm
The Pawnee Nation of Oklahoma
http://www.pawneenation.org

Index

24